Girlz Have Voices Books

The ANGRY
Girlchild

Girlz Have Voices Books

The ANGRY Girlchild

Tatenda Charles Munyuki

Darling Kind Publishing

THE ANGRY GIRLCHILD

Girlz Have Voices Books

First published in Zimbabwe in 2016.
Darling Kind Publishing
an imprint of Tatenda Charles Munyuki Publishing

Copyright © Tatenda Charles Munyuki 2016
Cover Illustration Copyright© Straightline Designz 2016
Cover illustration by Straightline Designz 2016

The moral rights of the author have been asserted.

ISBN   978 0 7974 7639 4

Printed and bound by Darling Kind Publishing,

Harare, Zimbabwe.

facebook.com/girlzhavevoices
facebook.com/tatendacmunyuki

Chapter One

Anna

It was a new world, or perhaps it was an old one made pretty by the flowers and the bees that buzzed around.

Being a girl was fun. The most powerful leaders in the free world were once girls too. It gave so much hope for the many girls out there. Anna Dana was one of those girls. Anna was eleven years old and her daddy always told her she was pretty. She loved Daddy so much and Daddy was the only parent she had. She also had aunts, Daddy's sisters who checked up on her here and there, but the person who mattered the most wasn't there. She missed her mummy sometimes.

Her parents had divorced when she was seven years old and Mummy had left her with Daddy. She didn't know why her mother didn't want her, but her daddy had told her that her mother was some kind of *witch*. Not like the good witches from her favourite Harry Potter books, but a selfish witch. Whenever Daddy spoke of Mummy, Anna could see the anger on his face. She always wondered if her mother was a real witch. *What had she done to Daddy for him to hate her so much?*

'Am I a little witch too? Will I become a little witch too?' Anna would ask herself day in, day out.

During the years she had been with Mummy, Mummy was never home. Mummy travelled a lot, but then she would return with lots of sweets, toys and clothes for her. People said she was a *border crosser*, who bought goods from South Africa and sold them in Zimbabwe.

Anna remembered meeting what her mother called *little uncles*. At that age, she didn't know what it meant, only that the little uncles came to visit when Daddy was away or at work. The little uncles were pretty too and they always brought her sweets and marshmallows. Oh God, did she love marshmallows.

Then one day her daddy had brought her marshmallows from work and she had told him his marshmallows were bigger than the ones the little uncles had brought her. Daddy had wanted to know who these little uncles were and when they came to the house. She had told him.

Now eleven years old, she knew who the little uncles were. Her aunts hadn't hidden that truth from her. The little uncles were Mummy's boyfriends. Daddy knowing about the little uncles had caused the divorce, she had been told. Her mother had told her that she was the reason Daddy was sending her away. Mummy told her that because she was that reason, she wasn't taking her along with her. She was leaving her with Daddy and she had been left with dear Daddy.

During the first days, she missed her mother awfully. Aunt Chiedza had come to stay with them for some time, doing what Mummy was supposed to do. At first, she didn't like Aunt Chiedza. Aunt Chiedza was too strict and she smelt funny. The freedom Anna had with Mummy was no longer there. Aunt Chiedza was always at home, making her do house chores, making her do homework and not buying her marshmallows. Most of all, Anna didn't like Aunt Chiedza because she didn't let her sleep late watching TV. When she complained to Daddy, Daddy would only laugh. He didn't even scold Aunt Chiedza for that.

At one time, she tried making Daddy and Aunt Chiedza hate each other, by telling each bad stories about the other. It had nearly worked until the day Aunt Chiedza spanked her and told her that little girls who lied were going to be spanked. She had told Daddy thinking he would be angry, but Daddy had said that spanking was part of life.

Hating Aunt Chiedza became something Anna was determined to do for the rest of her life. She didn't know how Aunt Chiedza could be serious one day, then with her friends around the house laughing and dancing. She had a habit of having her hair made every week, and one month she had had it coloured red. The day they became friends was one school holiday – after Aunt Chiedza took her to a salon and had her hair coloured red too. Anna had spent the whole holiday with her hair like that.

All of a sudden, after becoming cool friends with her aunt, Aunt Chiedza had to leave suddenly too. She said it was time for her to go to college. Anna had no idea what *college* was, except that it was the grownups school of some sort. She was now left with dear Daddy. Daddy had employed a maid to take care of her and the house as Aunt Chiedza used to do. The new maid was called Tanya – she called her Sisi Tanya. Sisi Tanya wasn't as strict as Aunt Chiedza was. Sisi Tanya was fun and talked a lot. She talked a lot. Anna sometimes thought she was the human form of the parrots she saw on TV. However, Sisi Tanya made her wash her own clothes. Aunt Chiedza had been strict, but she had never made her wash her own clothes.

'You are growing into a young lady,' Sisi Tanya had said. 'You should learn to do things like that by yourself.'

Sisi Tanya taught Anna a number of things. She taught her how to stitch and patch her clothes. She taught her how to cook and many things. With time, Anna loved Sisi Tanya.

School for Anna was fun, mainly because she was a very good student and the teachers loved her. She had a best friend in the name of Tino. Tino was this little girl who really loved to eat, and so she was round and bossy. Tino was her best friend because they had learned together at the same crèche and now at the same primary school. She loved Tino and Tino was a joker.

Tino liked to re-tell stories her big brother told her to her friends, and the stories, though absurd, were very funny. In class, it was either Tino or Anna who got the number one spot after the end of every term. Anna didn't like losing, so she worked hard on every lesson to get the better of Tino. Tino was a force to reckon with as she too worked hard on every lesson to get the best of her. The only differences between the two of them was perhaps that Tino lived with both her mummy and daddy, and that she was bigger than Anna. At the age of ten, everything in her life was great.

Anna smiled all the time, laughed all the time and was a happy girl. She was a happy girlchild.

Chapter Two

THE UNCLE WITH THE STICKY FINGERS

When Anna turned eleven years old, Daddy bought her a very pretty cellphone. He had a friend who sold phones called Jack. It was pink, had a huge pretty screen and, most of all, had all the best games she loved to play on his phone.

Jack often visited the house with Daddy, usually during the weekend. He was very tall, had this amazing light skin Anna didn't think men could have. The only person who had such light skin was Mummy. Mummy was extremely light-skinned. She had heard people calling her funny names like *yellowbone*. Uncle Jack, as he wanted to be called, was a yellowbone too. He had this beautiful car called a Benz, which was forever shiny and smiling.

From the looks of it, and Sisi Tanya's constant bragging, Uncle Jack had a lot of money. Whenever he visited the house, Anna would see him and Daddy carry these huge bags that had what they called golf sticks. The two would leave the house and Daddy would return late at night after she was asleep.

Sisi Tanya liked Uncle Jack very much and she had these funny looks and voice changes whenever she talked to him. Anna didn't know what it was, and when she asked her, Sisi Tanya would always laugh about it. Growing up a very active and agile girl, Sisi Tanya always bragged that she was very pretty and asked her if her extremely long hair had ever been cut. Anna barely remembered her hair being cut. Mummy had had long hair and had never cut hers as she had seen with her friends. Some of her friends would come to school with their hair cut at the beginning of every term, and at first, Anna didn't understand this. She had asked her mother why this was so.

'They are poor honey,' Mummy would say in her laughing syrupy voice. 'They don't have money to have it made like I do with yours.'

During her mother's days, the house would be filled with hair products that she sold or used, and she would often experiment with Anna's hair. After understanding this, Anna had stopped worrying about it and hoped she could share her mother's products with her friends so that they wouldn't have their hairs cut.

With long hair, her mother's yellowbone skin, and growing tall every day, she was indeed a very pretty girl. When Uncle Jack started visiting the house when Anna's daddy wasn't around, Sisi Tanya was very happy. He made excuses of why he had visited, bringing both of them goodies.

Then Sisi Tanya started noticing something she didn't like. She saw that Uncle Jack liked to play around with Anna very much, than he did with her. At first, she was a bit jealous seeing how they bonded. Then one day, after Uncle Jack visited, she went out to see someone who was knocking at the gate. As it was a hawker, she took some time there.

Five minutes later, she returned into the house to find Uncle Jack holding down Anna on his laps, his hands on her thighs, caressing them playfully.

'Please come here, Anna!' Sisi Tanya said in a voice so unlike her own. The look on her face had scared Anna.

'What? Uncle Jack is helping me try on the new shoes he brought me. Here, look?' Anna said raising her new sneakers happily.

'I said come here, damn it!' Sisi Tanya said again, fiercely this time.

Anna got up slowly, confused, holding her shoes.

'What's wrong?' Uncle Jack said standing up, with a weak smile.

'Please, can you leave now,' Sisi Tanya said to Uncle Jack.

'I was just helping her try her shoes on,' Uncle Jack said.

'It's okay. Please leave, now!' Sisi Tanya said as calmly as she could, pulling Anna to her side and hugging her protectively.

Uncle Jack stared her daggers and frowned. He walked away.

'And please only return when Mr Dana is around,' Sisi Tanya added.

Uncle Jack turned and gave her a dirty look. He left in his beautiful car fuming with anger. Sisi Tanya looked very angry for the rest of the day and Anna had no idea why. She eventually thought Sisi Tanya was jealous of her friendship with Uncle Jack.

Two days later, Uncle Jack had visited again. This time he brought with him a box of beautiful shoes and a new phone for Sisi Tanya. Sisi Tanya shocked Anna by throwing the things back at him and locked the door, shouting at him to go away. He left again, fuming.

That night when Mr Dana returned from work, Sisi Tanya approached him.

'I don't want to see Jack here again?' Sisi Tanya said.

Mr Dana stared at her confused. 'Why? What's wrong? What happened?'

'He has been coming over when you aren't around,' Sisi Tanya said.

'Why? You haven't told me this before?' Mr Dana said.

'He has been bringing me and Anna gifts. At first, I thought he liked me, but he doesn't. He likes Anna instead,' Sisi Tanya said.

Mr Dana laughed nervously. 'I don't see what's wrong. Everyone likes Anna. She is adorable,' he said proudly.

'I mean he likes Anna, as in *likes* Anna,' Sisi Tanya said angrily, more power in voice on the word *likes*.

'I don't know what you are on about, Tanya,' Mr Dana said, now a little frustrated. 'What are you really saying?'

'What I am saying is…' Sisi Tanya said, folding her hands. 'He likes fooling around with her, playing these games that makes him able to touch her. The other day, he had her on his laps, busy touching her all over her —'

'What?' Mr Dana shouted shocked.

Sisi Tanya repeated what she had said.

'Liar!' Mr Dana shouted. 'What are you trying to do? How can you say something like that about Jack?'

'I'm sorry, but he is a pervert,' Sisi Tanya said strongly. 'You must keep him away from Anna. So far away.'

'He is no pervert! He is a grown respectable man and friend,' Mr Dana replied angrily.

They argued for ten minutes as Anna heard, sitting in a corner in the kitchen, disturbed by the racket.

'Pack your bags and go right now!' Mr Dana shouted angrily.

He pushed Sisi Tanya to her room and forced her to pack as he watched. Anna cried silently, watching the *beast* that had become her dear daddy. She watched as Sisi Tanya was kicked out of the house into the night and told never to come back. It was a shocking experience for Anna who had no idea what was happening.

She barely slept that night and had baggy eyes the following morning when Daddy woke her up to get ready for school. He didn't look like the *Daddy* he was last night. He had a weak and caring smile on. Anna was scared even to ask what had happened to her beloved Sisi Tanya. She bathed and got ready for school.

In the middle of having breakfast, before leaving with Daddy, the door suddenly opened and in came Aunt Zena Maona. Behind her was Sisi Tanya. Aunt Zena was her mother's only sibling and big sister.

Aunt Zena rarely visited the house, but had once did so one day to check on Anna after she had had a nasty flu. Daddy had called her, asking her to check Anna's condition. Aunt Zena was a very successful woman. She was a doctor who had lots of money and lived alone at a very beautiful neighbourhood.

Although Mummy and Aunt Zena were both tall, Aunt Zena had shorter hair, less lighter skin and Mummy was far prettier than she was. She looked serious than Mummy did, carrying around a pair of reading glasses. Before Mummy had left, Aunt Zena used to visit, but now had only visited once when Sisi Tanya was there. She had liked Sisi Tanya and told her that if Anna ever needed anything, she didn't hesitate to get in touch with her.

When Aunt Zena arrived with Sisi Tanya, Daddy became his previous night's self again – becoming very angry. The previous night's argument continued, with Aunt Zena now involved.

'How can you believe such lies, Zena,' Daddy said. 'She is just a maid with a grudge because Jack didn't return her feelings.'

'I'm not lying,' Sisi Tanya said.

'Shut up, Tanya – adults are talking!' Daddy shouted at her.

'How well do you know this Jack?' Aunt Zena said to Daddy.

'For years. He and I have been business associates for years,' Daddy said defensively.

'Is he married? Does he have kids?' Aunt Zena asked.

Daddy shook his head. 'He doesn't and that doesn't mean anything at all.'

As the grownups argued, Anna just stared on. She didn't know why they were arguing and not taking notice of her standing right there.

'Let's ask Anna,' Sisi Tanya suddenly said, seeing the look of shock on her face.

'Tell us what happened, dear,' Daddy said smiling at her. 'It's okay, don't be afraid. Tell us the truth of what happened.'

Anna was unsure at first, but seeing the caring look on Daddy's face, she had told them how Uncle Jack had brought her new shoes and helped her put them on. She told them of the games they played together, taking pictures with his phone. Daddy's face turned icy with each word that came out of her mouth.

'What? Did I do anything naughty?' she asked innocently.

Daddy turned to Sisi Tanya. 'How dare you feed her lies?'

'That's the truth,' Sisi Tanya shouted back.

'Either way, whatever the case, I'm not leaving her here with you. She is coming to stay with me for a while,' Aunt Zena said, taking Anna's hand.

Daddy moved forward to stop her. 'She isn't going anywhere. Where were you when your sister left her with me? Now you want her?' he said fiercely.

'Please step aside. This won't do you any good to argue. You know if I really want to make it happen, it won't be good for you and your friend. You know the people I know,' Aunt Zena said sternly too.

Daddy frowned, but moved away slowly. Anna left the house with Aunt Zena, in her car that was driven by some man. Aunt Zena had her driver drive them to her school and promised her that she would pick her up after school.

Before long, Anna found herself being moved to Aunt Zena's huge house where she lived alone. She didn't have a husband and her only child was at college. At the house was the maid and the gardener. Aunt Zena had employed Sisi Tanya as her other maid. The other maid who was older was called Gamu.

During the first days at Aunt Zena's house, Anna spent most of her time with Sisi Gamu. She was so angry with Sisi Tanya that she didn't want to talk to her. She blamed her for being brought to the huge house that seemed like a lonely ghost house. She blamed her for Daddy being angry. She blamed her for everything.

Her other aunts – her father's sisters – especially Aunt Chiedza, visited the house demanding to see her. Words like *child abuse, child molestation* were thrown around.

Had she been child abused? Anna thought.

She told her friends at school and Tino had a lot to say.

'How did he touch you? What did he do to you?' Tino asked excitedly.

'Nothing. He just helped me put on the shoes, holding my legs,' Anna said to her, showing her.

'Child abuse!' Tino said.

'It wasn't!' Anna said, not liking the idea of being child abused. She remembered the kids on TV who had been child abused. She remembered their tears and sad faces.

'You were so,' Tino said.

Anna walked away angrily, ignoring her to go and play with the other girls.

Chapter Three

SHE CALLED ME NAMES

The longest week of Anna's life began on a Monday, and where else, but at school? She had had a frustrating weekend at her aunt's home and was very angry. Her Daddy had promised to come and see her that weekend, as he had promised the previous weekend on the new phone Aunt Zena had bought for her. The pink one from Daddy, which Uncle Jack had given him, had been sadly thrown away.

Daddy hadn't come to visit her, not even once. *Did Daddy not love her anymore?* She had tried calling him, to make sure he was coming, but his phone had kept on ringing, with no answer.

Sister Tanya had told her that he was perhaps busy, that being the reason he wasn't responding or coming by.

'Busy playing golf with Uncle Jack?' Anna had burst at her.

She already didn't want to talk to her, and her saying this only angered her more. She wished she could talk to someone else other than the maids.

Her Aunt Zena was indeed a busy person. Anna barely saw her during the week, even the weekends. School wasn't much fun anymore, mainly because Tino now had the habit of calling her names.

They were friends, indeed, but as time passed, with the pressure of being alone at home, Anna was beginning to call her names back.

'You are fat, Fatty fats Tino,' Anna said that Monday. She didn't understand why Tino was being nasty to her.

Tino didn't like to be called *fat*. She frowned at her. 'Don't call me that!' she screamed at her.

It was break time and the girls were busy playing at one side.

'And you stop calling me names,' Anna screamed back.

'Why are you screaming, you two?' one of their friends suddenly asked.

'She is calling me fat?' Tino said, frowning.

'And she is calling me *Child Abuse*,' Anna said frowning back.

'What is child abuse?' the friend asked, the other girls joining in.

'She was playing house with her uncle!' Tino said quickly.

'Definitely not!' Anna shouted back.

'You two should fight!' the other girls said excitedly.

'I will beat her,' Tino said fiercely.

'You won't!' Anna screamed back.

Tino advanced toward Anna and started pushing her. Her being huge and Anna being tall, it really did appear funny as the two struggled with each other. The other girls finally stopped them and break time was over before the two bickered again. When they returned to class, Anna tried to change her place of sitting to sit as far away as she could from Tino. This meant that she had to sit close to where the boys were. She made so much noise in her moving that their teacher, Mrs Huni, had to stop her.

'Anna, what's going on with you? Stop pulling that desk. It's making so much noise,' Mrs Huni shouted from her desk.

'I no longer want to sit with Tino, ma'am,' Anna said pulling her desk to make squeakier noises that irritated Mrs Huni.

Mrs Huni stood up in a flash. 'I said stop that!' she shouted at her.

Anna stopped and shrugged, folding her hands. The class laughed.

'What's going on here? Why don't you want to sit with your friend?' Mrs Huni asked.

'She is being mean to me. I don't want to sit with her ever,' Anna pouted and took her bag to move to the other side.

'You, Tino, what did you do to Anna?' Mrs Huni asked, staring hard at Tino like an owl.

'I did nothing, ma'am. She is just being funny,' Tino responded from where she was sitting.

'She is lying, ma'am,' Anna said.

'I'm not!' Tino replied equally.

'Okay, okay,' Mrs Huni raised her hands to stop them from arguing. 'No furniture is being rearranged. You, David, go and sit where Anna was sitting. Anna, go and sit where David was sitting. Take your things and switch, now – chop-chop!'

Anna and David changed sits as quickly as possible.

After school, things got heated when the girls were waiting to be picked up for home. Anna was waiting for the driver her aunt sent every day to pick her up. Tino waited for her brother to do the same.

A number of other pupils waited like them. One of the girls suddenly looked at Tino and grinned. She was called Sincere – a bundle of naughty as many in the class knew. Seeing Tino and Anna at opposite sides, frowning at each other, really did make her happy. She was jealous of their relationship and seeing these two at opposite sides tingled her insides.

'Tino, Anna said she will beat you up if you keep looking at her funny,' Sincere suddenly shouted.

Given the excuse to attack, Tino ambled over and pushed Anna away roughly. Anna collided into one of the waiting stone benches. It was very painful. The pain created an anger of its own. She moved furiously toward Tino and started propelling slaps at her. She was so emotional, her fury of slaps were unstoppable. Tino screamed at her – trying to return her own slaps, but Anna was too tall and vicious.

'Fight, fight, fight!' The other pupils who were nearby cheered and shouted, encouraging others to come and watch.

Pupils ran to the spot, pushing and nudging each other for a better view of the fight. Anna didn't stop hitting Tino. It was as if a demon had taken over her and all she wanted to do was hit, hit, and hit the fat out of Tino. Eventually, Tino did manage to hit back and sneak in a few slaps. The chaotic girls moved from one side, to the other, up and down. It was like a small circle that shifted every second, the other pupils creating the circle – shouting and jeering.

The two girls fighting were in their own world. They threw their hands at each other, scratched, screamed, and pulled at each other's hair and dresses. Anna's disadvantage was her long hair. It was easy to pull and so Tino pulled it every time she got the chance. Tino's disadvantage was that she was too short and so an easy target to slap down. Their clothes were being ripped apart, getting dirty with each second.

The Headboy and another boy prefect suddenly realized that this was getting out of hand, as both girls were now showing signs of a little blood and injuries. It was getting violent. They bullied themselves in.

'Move away, move away, now!' the Headboy shouted to the pupils in his way.

He had to push them aside as they weren't listening. He was very tall and bulky, one of the school's rugby players. He made his way to the circle easy enough, the other prefect behind him. They tried as best as they could to hold back the girls with the noisy crowd ringing in their ears.

Anna slapped Tino, repeatedly, as the Headboy tried pulling her back. She was even crying. It was difficult to see who was coming out on top of the fight. With Tino's dark skin and hugeness, she looked better than Anna, who unfortunately to her yellowbone skin, now looked very pink and beaten. A teacher finally arriving at the spot of the fight was what really stopped it. Both girls were pulled to opposite ends. Both were crying and extremely dingy. Both girls had their uniforms torn in more than one place.

'Come with me, right now!' the teacher said, gesturing at the two and the prefects.

The four followed the teacher towards the school's buildings. The other pupils watched as they went. As the teacher walked away in brisk steps, the four suddenly realized where he was heading. Both girls' hearts started beating fast. They knew they were in big trouble. A minute later, they reached the Headmistress' office. The teacher ordered the girls and boys to wait by the waiting benches. He disappeared into the office to what seemed like ages.

Anna and Tino sat as far away from each other as possible. The Headboy and the other prefect sat in the middle, wondering if they too were in trouble. The Headboy looked at the girls. They looked like they were in Grade Six, because he knew almost every grade seven and these weren't grade sevens. He stared at Anna more. He couldn't help noticing that apart from looking like a scarecrow right then, she was very pretty. Anna was noticeably tall, which made her look older. He looked at Tino and wondered why these girls had been fighting at all. It was unheard of, girls fighting at the school.

'Why were you two fighting?' he couldn't help asking.

The door to the Headmistress' office suddenly opened. The teacher peeped his head out.

'You two, come in,' he said to the prefects. The prefects did as asked.

At both ends of the benches, Anna and Tino sat frowning, trying extremely hard no to look at each other. They both knew their friendship was over. Five minutes later, the door opened and the boys came from it looking very serious.

'You two, come in,' the teacher said to the girls.

The girls looked up at him, wide-eyed. They both felt very scared. Both had never been in the Headmistress' office before.

'Girls!' the teacher said in a stern voice.

None of the girls looked like she was getting up. Each waited for the other to be the first to stand. The teacher saw that none was going to stand readily. He shook his head and returned into the office. Not more than a minute later, the door was opened and the Headmistress stood at it. She was called Mrs Kapfuti and was a huge woman who had a scary hairstyle – a weave – and wore glasses. The two girls were up in a flash, ready to comply.

Inside the office, the girls started by being timid, but as fingers started to get pointed at each other, the girls suddenly became noisy.

'She hit me first,' Tino said.

'She started it. She pushed me and I got hurt,' Anna shouted defensively.

'Where is this behaviour coming from? Who told you that girls must fight?' the Headmistress said staring hard at the two like an angry owl.

The teacher stood at the nearby sofa, watching over. The two girls shrugged, pouted and said nothing.

'Why were you fighting?' the Headmistress asked.

'She was calling me names,' Anna was the first to say it.

'I was not!' Tino lied through her teeth.

'Yes you were – you were calling me names!' Anna spat back at her.

'Silence!' the Headmistress shouted. Silence followed. 'Whatever name-calling or not, that doesn't give you the right to be fighting. I will not have such behaviour at my school. This isn't a secondary institution where you have girls menstruating and having sudden moods.'

The girls were silent and looked on feeling the Headmistress' eyes drill into them.

'What is menstruating?' Anna's curiosity suddenly got the best of her.

Chapter Four

JUST LIKE FIRE

The Headmistress had let them off with a warning. It was a stern warning that had taken twenty whole minutes, being educated about the dangers of being naughty girls and how naughty girls ended up in life. Anna knew talking to Tino was going to be next to difficult after what had just happened. Her driver for home had been very stunned to see her looking like she had been vomited from the mouth of a beast. She now had a female driver and the driver hadn't asked what had happened, but Sisi Tanya surely asked.

'What happened to you?' Sisi Tanya asked a little disturbed.

Anna shrugged helplessly. 'I was fighting.'

'You were what?' Sisi Tanya asked shocked.

'Tino was calling me names. I couldn't help it – I beat her,' Anna said, not daring to look at her.

Sisi Tanya looked her up and down and shook her head. 'What is really going on with you, Anna? Now you are fighting at school?'

'She was calling me names. She was calling me child abuse,' Anna said pouting.

'She was calling you what?' Sisi Tanya asked.

'Child abuse,' Anna said.

'Why would she call you that?' Sisi Tanya asked stunned.

'I told her what happened to me and then she started making fun of me saying I was child abused. I told her that it wasn't true. It's not true, right?'

'Oh my God. Why in the world would you go around telling

your friends about something like that?' Sisi Tanya frowned at her. 'Come on, quick – let's get you cleaned up. We wouldn't want your aunt to suddenly return and see you like that.'

Sisi Tanya pulled Anna to her room where she had her change before taking a bath – to deal with the torn uniform. Bathing for Anna was tricky. The scratches and wounds she had got from the fight itched and stung her. Sisi Tanya watched over her as she bathed and made sure she did actually wash herself. Afterwards, Sisi Tanya put disinfectant and two small bandages on them.

'Don't tell your Aunt what happened. If she asks, tell her you got hurt playing,' she said.

Anna nodded. She didn't want to get into trouble with Aunt Zena. She hoped she was at home with Daddy, so she could tell him all about her worries. However, it seemed like Daddy didn't want to see her. *Didn't Daddy love her anymore?*

To Anna's surprise, Aunt Zena did return early that day. She had dinner with her, as the maids had their dinner in the kitchen. The two of them, in the huge dining room, really did feel weird for Anna. This was the first time they were having dinner as only the two of them.

'How is school?' Aunt Zena asked, eating. Her plate was full of various vegetables and pasta.

Anna stared at her plate for a second. This was the second time she was seeing her eat food like this. Being asked about school made her think of the fight.

'It is okay,' she lied, looking at her plate. There was a variety of meat in her meals these days. She thought sometimes she was going to get as fat as Tino, because she wasn't used to eating like this. Her plate had fish, chicken and beef. She had no idea what to eat, what not to eat. She ate all of it.

'What happened to you?' Aunt Zena said studying her bandages.

Anna looked up at her scared of being found out. She looked back down. 'I fell at school, playing around.'

Aunt Zena studied her for a while, and later thought nothing of it. She continued eating. 'Are you prepared for your grade seven exams?'

Anna looked up at her confused. 'I am in grade six,' she said to her.

'I know. But are you studying hard, getting ready for them?' Aunt Zena asked in a firm voice.

'I read hard and get the best scores in class,' Anna said proudly.

'That's good,' Aunt Zena smiled weakly. 'At least you are different. Your mother was never one for books.'

Anna looked at her – long and curious. 'Where is Mummy?'

'She must be somewhere around,' Aunt Zena said. 'Who knows with your mother? When was the last time you saw her?'

Anna suddenly felt sad. 'I don't remember. She doesn't want to see me. She hates me.'

'I'm sure in her own twisted ways, she loves you,' Aunt Zena said smiling weakly at her.

'And Daddy? He promised me he'd come and see me. He lied to me. He doesn't want to see me at all,' Anna said angrily.

Aunt Zena tried to think of something to say, but couldn't. She knew this little niece of hers was her responsibility now and if she was going to grow up into half the decent woman her little sister – Anna's mother – wasn't, she was the responsible aunt and possibly her best hope.

'Everything is going to be okay, Anna. Don't worry yourself about such things. I'm here for you.'

They ate in silence for a while.

'Why don't you eat meat?' Anna suddenly asked, staring at her plate again.

'I'm a vegetarian now,' Aunt Zena smiled at her curiosity, which looked cute on her.

'What is that?' Anna asked.

'Someone who doesn't eat meat. I only eat vegetables now,' Aunt Zena explained to her.

'No meat at all? Have you always been a vegita– vegitu– a vegie?' Anna said, not able to pronounce the word properly.

Aunt Zena laughed. 'No. I have eaten meat before, for a long time. My doctor advised me to lay low on meat for a few months, for my diet,' she said. 'You do know what a diet is, right?'

Anna nodded. 'Yes, I do, but aren't you a doctor? You have a doctor?'

Aunt Zena giggled. 'Even doctors have doctors too, dear. Mine told me to diet and that's why I don't eat meat now.'

'Oh,' Anna said, scanning her body structure.

Like her mummy, Aunt Zena was a fine boned woman too. She could easily become huge if she wanted to. However, Anna didn't see why she would need to be on diet because she didn't look like a Tino or fat at all. Perhaps diet meant a whole lot of different things for the grownups, she thought.

Going to school the following day was a difficult thing for Anna. It meant seeing Tino. When she reached school, she discovered that that was the least of her problems. Pupils were talking about the fight. Their class teacher wasn't pleased at all. She asked them to come in front of the class.

'How can you disgrace my class like that?' Mrs Huni said angrily. 'You are going to sit on the floor in that naughty corner until break time. The both of you.'

Anna and Tino were forced to sit in the naughty corner as the class laughed at them. The naughty corner was a very embarrassing place to be and they had to sit with their legs crossed, holding their skirts onto the dirty floor to avoid any Peeping Toms from looking down on them. It was a long two hours on the floor and when break time came, both girls rose cramped and feeling very dirty. They both wore frowns and shrugged continuously.

Because Tino's friends were Anna's friends, break time was a very uncomfortable process. That meant there had to be a division of friends. Because Tino had a lot of food, great and sweet food during break time, Anna found herself very alone. She was in fact sitting alone. Life suddenly became terrible for her. At home, she was alone. *Now at school too?*

What had she done wrong to deserve all this bad luck? She thought continuously. She felt angry with both her parents and her friends. She tried to calm herself, telling herself continuously that she didn't care about Tino and the other girls who had left her alone.

She could make new friends. The boys liked her. She would make new friends with the boys.

After break, the class had to go out for scouts and games under the old and broad Muhacha trees. Just as before break had been trying for both Anna and Tino, this time it was difficult for Anna who continued being alone at the girls' sector. It seemed like Tino had mobilized every girl in the class to leave Anna alone as some form of punishment.

Anna left and went to play with the boys, who were more than happy to have her there. When the teacher finally noticed this oddity, she called Anna from the boys and commanded her to join the girls.

'But they don't want to play with me, Mrs Huni,' Anna complained.

'I don't want to hear that again. You girls, and you Anna, get yourselves together and make it work!' Mrs Huni shouted.

Anna and the girls grudgingly joined together and started going through the routines. During the routines, it was clumsy work because everyone kept avoiding Anna. The ball was passed around, jumping her many times as if she wasn't there. Anna got angry and suddenly rushed into one of the girls. The girl fell and hurt herself. Although it was a minor scratch, nothing to write home about, the girl made it such a big deal and started howling. After a minute or two of making the girl stop howling, Mrs Huni turned and picked up a stick.

'Hold out your hand, Anna,' she ordered.

'Why?' Anna said curiously, as the other students watched.

'I said hold out your hand. You are being a difficult child. Hold out your hand, now!' Mrs Huni shouted.

Anna held out her hand and it was struck hard. She screamed.

'Again!' Mrs Huni shouted.

Scared, Anna held out her hand and it was struck again.

'If you become naughty again, it will be worse for you. Understand?'

Anna shook her head with shock and a few tears. The teacher turned and walked away. Anna turned to the girls who giggled and sneered at her. She felt a rush of uncontrolled anger. She turned and looked at Mrs Huni. She picked up a *hacha* and threw it at the teacher without thinking. The *hacha* hit her perfectly on the back.

Mrs Huni turned stunned. She saw Anna standing there angry.

'F*** you, Mrs Huni!' she said without even blinking.

The class was shocked, the teacher even more so.

Mrs Huni looked like she was swelling and about to explode into different shades of anger. 'What did you say?' she could barely breathe.

'You heard me,' Anna said folding her hands.

The other children stared on, not believing their ears. *Had Anna just used the forbidden f-word with the teacher?* They looked very awed and worried. Even Tino looked worried and felt bad. Whatever came next, all of them knew nothing good was going to come out of it.

Anna and Tino were in the Headmistress' office for the second time in two days. In the office was the Headmistress, sitting behind her desk with a very worried look.

Also in it was Mrs Huni and Aunt Zena. Aunt Zena didn't look pleased at all. She looked very thoughtful than worried.

'Dr Maona, you can understand why I had to call you because of this,' the Headmistress said in an ever-polite voice. Aunt Zena was a very respectable woman in society. It was a wonder she was related to this little rascal.

'I understand. Thank you for calling me,' Aunt Zena said.

'I had called her father, but surprisingly, he told me Anna was now your responsibility. Is that true?' the Headmistress was curious.

Aunt Zena nodded. 'Yes, she lives with me now. What really happened?'

The Headmistress sighed for a while. 'Well, yesterday Anna and her friend here were brought in after lunch after being involved in a huge fight. I let them off with a warning. I doubt if that was the right decision, because today Anna threw a stone at her teacher here and used the f-word insulting her.'

'It wasn't a stone, it was —'

'Shush, Anna!' Aunt Zena said immediately, sternly staring at her.

Anna pouted and shrugged. She was already in trouble, but she had not stoned the teacher. Mrs Huni had lied.

'That is very bad for a girl her age to be doing such things. You understand what I mean?' the Headmistress said.

Aunt Zena nodded. 'I understand,' she said, staring hard at Anna. *What was going on with this girl?* 'You told me you fell yesterday.'

'I'm sorry I lied, but she was calling me names and I –' Anna tried to say.

'Does that mean you have to fight? Is that what your father taught you?' Aunt Zena was slowly getting angry. 'And now you are stoning teachers and calling them – using the f-word?'

'She hit me for no reason, and, and… she was calling me child abuse,' Anna said in tears and in an uncontrollable voice full of emotions.

'I'm sorry, you said she called you what?' the Headmistress asked.

'She called me child abuse,' Anna said sobbing.

'I did no such thing!' Mrs Huni protested heatedly.

'Tino…' Anna sobbed. 'Tino called me child abuse.'

The others stared at Tino who suddenly felt very guilty.

'Why would you call her that?'

'It was only a joke after she told me about her Uncle Jack,' Tino said defensively.

Aunt Zena suddenly knew what was going on and understood everything.

The Headmistress must have understood too because she suddenly asked Mrs Huni and Tino to leave, remaining with Anna and her aunt. Aunt Zena explained what had happened to Anna and her sudden relocation to her custody and home. Anna was told to wait outside. She left the grownups to talk.

When her Aunt appeared later, she was asked to go and take her backpack for home.

Chapter Five

LiTTLe RASCAL

Between a parent and the child, a vertical relationship is complementary and involves an attachment to someone with greater social power and knowledge. Aunt Zena didn't hold back when they reached home. Sisi Tanya was told to join them.

'Fighting at school? You are a girl for crying aloud. Girls don't fight,' Aunt Zena said angrily. 'Was this what you were teaching her?' The question was directed at Sisi Tanya.

Sisi Tanya didn't respond, but only shook her head. She was ashamed of what Anna had done that day.

'You are very lucky your Headmistress respected me enough not to expel you away from school,' Aunt Zena said shaking her head.

'What is to happen to her now?' Sisi Tanya asked.

'She will return to school after a week. I asked her Headmistress for some time so she could see a doctor and get herself sorted out,' Aunt Zena said.

'But I am not sick,' Anna said.

'Some kind of doctor called a child psychiatrist, who talks to children,' Aunt Zena said softly.

'A week without going to school?' Anna was shocked.

'You should have thought about that before you threw a stone at the teacher and called her names,' Aunt Zena said and left the room.

The room was tense with only Sisi Tanya and Anna.

'You threw a stone at the teacher?' Sisi Tanya suddenly said angrily too.

'It was not a stone, it was a *hacha*,' Anna said defensively.

'Either way, how could you do that and use such words, at your teacher for crying out loud?' Sisi Tanya wasn't letting her off the hook.

Everything Anna did was reflected from her by Aunt Zena. This was very bad indeed. She was afraid she was going to be suddenly fired for not preventing this. She knew she had a week to try to make this right.

The following day, Anna felt odd not going to school on a school day. It remained just that, because living in a neighbourhood or house where you saw nothing, but the people you saw in it every day, made no difference – being a school day or not.

By breakfast time, she had no idea what to do with herself. She helped Sisi Tanya do chores. Sisi Tanya was happy they were now on speaking terms. She kept Anna busy.

As Anna's chores were in the living room where the huge TV was always on, she did them watching the TV. On it was a daytime drama about a family. The more she watched it, the more she felt lost. The family on the TV looked so happy. She wondered if her own family had ever been that happy.

Her thoughts went from her daddy to her mummy, then back again in a full circle. *How long was she going to live at this huge house, lonely and bored?* She wished she had more answers.

Was her daddy ever going to come to see her? Did he know that she had been in trouble at school? The stress she was feeling was more than she had felt when Mummy had left. Then, she knew she had Daddy – and for a while Aunt Chiedza. Now Daddy no longer wanted her. Her friend no longer wanted her. All she had now was Aunt Zena and Sisi Tanya. She felt like a lost girl, a *Patie Pan*.

Around lunch, the driver who used to pick her up from school came to take the maids to the local shopping center for some shopping for the household stuff. Anna refused to be left alone at home and went with them. Sisi Tanya thought it wise afraid of what Anna would do being left alone. With the level of mischief Anna was currently at, Sisi Tanya didn't want to risk it.

Being at a shopping mall, where many people were, made Anna feel like not going to school that day was a blessing. She walked around on her own after promising Sisi Tanya that she would appear here and then, and not leave the shop without them. Walking around the shop was fun, until she finally ran into a schoolgirl wearing a uniform. She was roughly her age. She was from a school Anna didn't know and with her was her mother. They looked very happy together, the girl carrying a bunch of assorted candy. Tino used to come to school with such candy and boast about it. Anna knew it was very expensive candy. The other kids' mothers wouldn't dare buy such candy or sweets for they thought it cost too much.

Anna remembered Mummy bringing her such candy and how she missed it. She wished she were this kid, enjoying some time with her mother. At another spot, she saw a boy – younger than she was – in another uniform she didn't recognize. The boy had his daddy with him and looked very excited. She remembered her own daddy.

Knowing both her parents were out there and she didn't get to have what these kids had made her very angry.

Sisi Tanya was glad when Anna finally showed up at the till where their groceries were being calculated and being put into paper bags. Sisi Gamu had the money to pay for the things and she was helping the shop assistant pack. Anna had never seen so much groceries being bought at one time in her life. She was now fully aware that Aunt Zena had a lot of money.

As they made their way out of the shop, with the security person at the entrance checking them, he finished and suddenly stared at Anna.

'Can you please open your pocket?' he said at Anna.

Anna refused and moved behind Sisi Tanya.

Sisi Tanya was stunned by such behaviour and forced Anna to

empty her pockets. 'Are you kidding me?'

Anna looked guilty. With all these groceries, she didn't think she would be caught.

'Please stand aside, ma'am,' the security guard said heatedly, using his hand to wave to another guard.

Anna and Sisi Tanya stood at one side – Sisi Tanya looking very angry. The security guard said something to the other guard who left right away.

Sisi Gamu stood there angrily. 'Anna, what is the meaning of this?' she asked.

'I'm sorry, I didn't know I had it in my pocket,' Anna said without looking at her.

'You didn't know you had two bars of chocolate in your pocket?' the guard said angrily.

If the kid wasn't as young as she was and a girl, he would have started beating her by now for trying to steal from the shop. However, the amount of groceries they had bought were too much for the guard wisely to hold back.

The other guard suddenly arrived with a man in a suit. He was the manager of the shop.

'Is it true that the girl tried to steal chocolate?' the manager asked the guard, looking at the maids and Anna.

The guard nodded. 'Yes, sir.'

The manager stared at the groceries and then the maids. 'I'm sorry, but what is going on?'

'I'm so sorry, sir, but the girl here seems to have developed sticky fingers. I'm so sorry,' Sisi Gamu apologized.

'What have you got to say about yourself girl?' the manager said staring at Anna.

Anna started dripping tears. 'I saw the other kids… with their mummy… I just thought… I am so sorry,' she sobbed.

The manager looked around and saw that people near the tills were suddenly taking notice of this. He looked at the maids and noted that none of them could be Anna's parent.

'Where are her parents? We should talk to them,' he said.

Sisi Tanya groaned. Yet another problem on a day after. Sisi

Gamu frowned and produced her phone.

'Let me give you her aunt's number,' she said producing her expensive looking phone that had the guards stare at her with jealously and envy.

They didn't know of a maid who could afford such a phone on a basic salary. Sisi Gamu gave the number to the manager who had produced his own phone.

'Whom do I say I want to speak to?' the manager said.

'Dr Maona,' Sisi Gamu said.

The manager looked up confused. He then looked at the groceries, then at Anna. 'You work for Dr Maona?' he asked Sisi Gamu.

'Yes,' Sisi Gamu said. 'This is her niece.'

'Oh,' the manager said. He looked up in thought, and then pocketed his phone. 'Let us not bother the Dr with such a silly juvenile matter. Let's just say you pay for the chocolates and we forget about it?'

Sisi Gamu's face lit up in gratitude. 'Thank you so much, sir,' she said producing money for the chocolates Anna had tried to steal.

On the drive back home, Anna had the tongue-lashing of a lifetime from Sisi Gamu about little girls who stole things from shops.

'You are very lucky, very, very lucky your aunt is a well-known person. You'd have gone to jail.'

'Jail?' Anna said shocked. She knew what she had done was very serious.

'Yes, that is where thieves belong,' Sisi Gamu said heatedly.

'But I'm not a thief,' Anna said shrugging.

'After what you tried to do, I can only wonder,' Sisi Gamu said looking away.

'Your aunt is going to be very angry about this,' Sisi Tanya said.

'You are going to tell her?' Anna said, scared.

'This is getting serious. She has to deal with you seriously,' Sisi Tanya said.

Chapter Six

THE PRETTY LADY

Anna was confused when Aunt Zena didn't talk to her about the shoplifting thing. For a second, she thought Sisi Tanya hadn't told her.

'I told her last night,' Sisi Tanya told Anna.

Anna was even more scared. *Why had Aunt Zena not shouted at her as Sisi Gamu had done? Was Aunt Zena fed up of her too just like Mummy and Daddy?* Spending the day at home made her think a lot. Watching TV wasn't fun anymore. It was only watchable after lunch, which was the time she often arrived from school. If Aunt Zena chased her away for being naughty, she wondered who would take her next.

Aunt Zena arrived in the early evening that day. Having been waiting for the sound of her car, Anna dashed for her room upstairs. She didn't want to see Aunt Zena, afraid of her fate.

The door to her room was opened ten minutes later. Aunt Zena peeped in. Anna looked up at her.

'Good evening, Anna,' she said with a weak smile.

'Good evening, Aunt Zena,' Anna said in a soft voice.

Aunt Zena opened the door wide. 'Here is someone I brought by to talk to you. This is my friend, Mrs Apter,' she said.

Mrs Apter suddenly appeared from behind Aunt Zena. She was very tall and pretty. She was a Caucasian woman with blond hair. Anna had never seen a Caucasian lady with that kind of hair so close, except on TV.

Aunt Zena closed the door as she left. Anna was left with Mrs Apter. She felt very uneasy in her presence.

'Hi, Anna, can I please sit?' Mrs Apter said, gesturing at the bed where Anna was.

Anna had lost her voice. She just nodded.

'Thank you,' Mrs Apter said sitting down. She looked around the room. 'Nice room you have here. Are those novels?'

Anna nodded again, still not finding her voice.

Mrs Apter stood up, walked over to the small bookshelf where Anna's books were. 'Harry Potter, Twilight, Nancy Drew, Xclusive Zone Angels, NACH,' Mrs Apter said reading the titles of the books one by one. 'Nice, you have read all of them?'

Anna was a bit surprised that this pretty lady was interested in her books. She nodded.

'Which one is your favourite?' Mrs Apter asked.

'Naa —' Anna finally found her voice. 'I loved the Harry Potters, but for now it's *NACH*.'

'NACH, hmmm,' Mrs Apter said. 'The Adventures of Chenai, Amanda, Nathan and Hama.'

'The Adventures of Nathan Amanda Chenai and Hama. You know about them?' Anna was indeed surprised. A grownup knowing a children's book was a surprise to her.

'I do,' Mrs Apter returned to sit on the bed with one of the NACH books with her. 'I have a daughter younger than you are, called Amanda and she loves the books.'

'They are fun books,' Anna said a little excited, watching her aunt's friend. 'Mrs Apter —'

'Please call me Aunt Rhoda,' Mrs Apter smiled at her.

'Your name is Rhoda too?' Anna asked surprised.

'You know of another Rhoda?' Aunt Rhoda said surprised.

'One of my aunts is called Rhoda,' Anna said. 'She is my daddy's cousin sister.'

'Ahh,' Aunt Rhoda said smiling. 'That's cool. What did you want to ask me?'

'I wanted to ask why Aunt Zena made you talk to me,' Anna said curiously.

'I'm a big fan of children. I like talking to children,' Aunt Rhoda said smiling warmly.

'Is it because of the fight, or the teacher or the shop?' Anna was curious on which crime she was going to answer for.

'I am more interested in you – Anna,' Aunt Rhoda said without changing her smile. 'Tell me, how do you feel being here?'

Anna stared at Aunt Rhoda. *Could she trust this pretty lady?* Aunt Rhoda had such a welcoming calm face. She had no choice, but to trust her. 'I miss home and Daddy.'

'What do you miss about home?' Aunt Rhoda asked.

'Everything, especially Daddy. I miss him lots,' Anna said sadly.

'What about your mother? Don't you miss your mother too?'

Anna shook her head. 'Not as much. Mummy left us a long time ago, plus Mummy was never at home.'

'Do you love your mummy?' Aunt Rhoda asked. Her smile didn't fade.

Anna thought about it. 'I don't know. She is my mummy.'

'Do you love your daddy?' Aunt Rhoda asked.

'Yes, I did,' Anna quickly said.

'You did?' Aunt Rhoda said. 'What about now?'

'I don't like him. He lied to me and he never came as he promised,' Anna said bitterly.

'Do you love your aunt?' Aunt Rhoda asked.

Anna nodded. 'She is a great aunt. A lot people know her. She is cool.'

Aunt Rhoda smiled more. 'Do you like staying here?'

Anna shook her head. 'It's so boring and huge. I am the only one here.'

'I know what you mean. It is a huge house with no one to play with. Will it be cool if you had more people to play with here?'

'Yah, it would be fun. There are so many places we can play at,' Anna said in an excited tone.

'Why don't you ask your friends to come over?' Aunt Rhoda asked.

'They live so far away from here,' Anna told her, 'and I don't have friends anymore.'

'Why is that?' Aunt Rhoda asked politely.

Anna told her about the fight and the teacher.

'So you and Tino can't make up?'

Anna shook her head. She wasn't going to forgive Tino for what she had done. 'Sisi Tanya told me that Tino isn't a good friend. She told me to make new friends.'

'But Tino won't let you?' Aunt Rhoda said. Anna nodded. 'You are not friends with Tino because she called you names. What did she call you?'

'She called me *child abuse*,' Anna said angrily.

'What do you think child abuse means?' Aunt Rhoda asked.

'It means I slept with Uncle Jack, she said,' Anna said as if irritated by the thought.

'You, yourself, what do you think it means?' Aunt Rhoda asked.

Anna stared at her confused. She shook her head. Aunt Rhoda placed a hand on hers with a caring soft touch.

'Child abuse is when an older person takes advantage of you, a kid, and forces you to do things kids aren't supposed to do. This is like hitting you, working you hard like a slave, causing you stress and harm, touching you at your private places or just touching you as if they are touching someone older. It doesn't matter who it is, be it a man or woman.'

Anna understood what she was saying. 'Was I child abused?'

Aunt Rhoda nodded sadly. 'When your father's friend, Jack, played with you, with games which he could touch you and your body like that, that was abuse. It's sick and isn't allowed. People go to jail for doing things like that.'

'So I was child abused?' Anna looked at her shocked. She couldn't believe her Uncle Jack was a sick man to child abuse her. 'Did I do something wrong for him to abuse me?'

Aunt Rhoda squeezed her hand. 'Not at all, dear. You're growing up and I have to say you have all the signs of growing up into a very pretty young lady. There are men out there with sick minds who will look at you funny, want to do things like what Jack was doing. It's not your fault or anyone's that you are pretty. No one should ever abuse anyone. It's insane, evil and illegal. You have to be very aware of such people as you grow up. Even boys too may want to abuse you, even girls. It's not your fault. It's their fault and they should never be allowed to get away with it.' She hugged Anna close to her.

'What should I do?' Anna sobbed.

'You are lucky to have an aunt who cares very much about you, even when your mummy and daddy aren't around. You don't have your parents around and it's not your fault as well. It's their fault not caring about such a beautiful young thing as yourself. Please don't blame yourself, but it is time to grow up fast. You must learn to control your temper, Anna. Your temper must not control you.'

Anna nodded, still sobbing. She didn't know why she felt so bad.

'There is no need to fight at school or call teachers names. Make friends and be happy. Be a kid and enjoy everything around you.'

Chapter Seven

New Anna

From that day, Aunt Rhoda became one of Anna's favourite people. She felt safe now knowing that her aunt and Aunt Rhoda were around to protect her. From the following day, the whole of Friday was enjoyable being at home. She did what Aunt Rhoda had told her. She had fun like a kid and spent the day exploring her aunt's huge house.

Amongst the many things she found, she found a small playhouse that was old. She thought it belonged to Aunt Zena's child who was now at grownup's school. She loved redecorating the place that she forgot to go home to eat.

Sisi Tanya found her an hour later looking very worried. 'You just don't go out like that without telling someone where you are. I thought something had happened to you.'

'*Mukoma* Fawo knew where I was,' Anna said. Mukoma Mufaro was the gardener. She called him *Fawo*.

'Yes, he is the one who told me. Still, listen to what I am saying. Promise me you'll tell me where you are going. This place is too huge to monitor you all the time,' Sisi Tanya said sternly.

'I promise, Sisi Tanya,' Anna said annoyed.

Sisi Tanya was always stern nowadays. She worried a lot about things Anna didn't think were worth worrying about.

The following morning, Aunt Zena didn't leave for work as early as she did. She did in fact go to the garden to do a little gardening where the flowers were. She looked funny in a straw hat and overalls.

Anna didn't know why Aunt Zena would do any gardening when Mukoma Fawo was there.

'Why are you doing this?' she finally asked.

'I like doing it. It keeps me calm and relaxed,' Aunt Zena smiled at her.

Anna went over to help her. As they weeded the flowers and whatever Aunt Zena was doing to them, Aunt Zena told her the names of each flower. Anna was surprised she knew so much about flowers and that there were so many of them. She tried to memorize them and saying out their names trying to impress her.

'What do you think about changing schools? Are you okay if I transfer you to another school that is closer to the house?' Aunt Zena suddenly asked.

Anna had her eyes wide open. 'Really? That would be cool,' she said. She couldn't imagine how happy she would be going to a school that had no Tino or an angry teacher waiting for her. 'I'd love that. That would be awesome!'

Aunt Zena laughed. 'Perhaps one day you'll become a doctor like me.'

'I don't think so,' Anna frowned. 'Doctors are busy people and I am lazy. I don't like blood too.'

Aunt Zena had thought it would be hard approaching the little girl with the subject about changing schools and was surprised at the excitement it brought out of Anna. She laughed some more.

'What do you want to be when you grow up?'

'I want to be Bill Gates,' Anna said so confidently.

Aunt Zena laughed some more. 'Do you even know who that is?'

Anna smiled. 'Daddy said Bill Gates is the richest person in the world,' she said proudly.

'Bill Gates is a man, young lady,' Aunt Zena said giggling.

'Oh,' Anna felt silly. 'Okay – then when I grow up I want to be Hillary Clinton.'

Aunt Zena laughed some more. 'That, you can be, my dear

child. That you can be. With the girlchild of today, you can be what you want to be. The sky is the limit.'

www.ingramcontent.com/pod-product-compliance
Lightning Source LLC
Chambersburg PA
CBHW050917120626
46552CB00004B/1627